JANELL CANNON

VOYAGER BOOKS • HARCOURT, INC.

Orlando Austin New York San Diego Toronto London

With appreciation to David K. Faulkner, entomologist, and
David G. Gordon, author and bug lover, for keeping the facts straight;

and to Taffy Cannon, author; Jeannette Larson, editor; and Judythe Sieck, designer,
for their help in making all the puzzle pieces fit.

And thanks to these authors for writing: *The Compleat Cockroach: A Comprehensive Guide to the Most Despised (And Least Understood) Creature on Earth* by David G. Gordon;
The Ants by Bert Hölldobler and Edward O. Wilson; and
Play with Your Food by Joost Elffers.

This one's for Jani

Far below the great forest canopy lies a shadowy world that many insects call home. Among the damp clutter of fallen leaves and branches, leaf-cutting ants toil all day while large cockroaches await their evening search for food.

One cockroach had looked like all the others—until a close call with a hungry toad. In his wild escape from the toad's sticky tongue, he had twisted one of his fine long wings. Since then everyone called him Crickwing.

Crickwing despised his nickname, and he avoided hearing it by staying far away from the other creatures. He would sneak out to find his food when the night was darkest, knowing that the forest was crawling with predators even worse than ravenous toads.

The forest seemed much less fearsome whenever Crickwing found a nice pile of tasty leaves, roots, and petals. He took comfort in their bright colors and interesting shapes, and he often built sculptures from them before he ate them. When he was busy playing with his food, he could almost forget the pain in his crooked wing.

One night Crickwing created his most wonderful sculpture ever. He was so absorbed in his work that he didn't hear the soft footsteps behind him. . . .

Pow! Swoosh! A sharp-eyed monkey clobbered Crickwing and swiped his sculpture.

Crickwing dived for cover. "I only let him get away with that because he's so big," he grumbled, cowering under a rotten log.

Crickwing hid until the next night, when hunger drove him out to search for a meal. But as soon as he had added the final flower petal to his dinner, an enormous, scaly lizard nearly gulped him down. Crickwing dodged, and the lizard took off with his edible artwork.

"Another masterpiece—ruined!" Crickwing panted. "I'm starving and my wing aches. I don't know if I can take this much longer."

The next night things got even worse. An ocelot pounced and nearly crushed Crickwing. When he darted away, the ocelot scooped him up in her massive paw and threw him high into the air.

"Oh nooooo!" Crickwing wailed. "Not again!"

When he landed, Crickwing scrambled about in a panic and leaped into a crevice under a stone, where he collapsed in angry tears.

"I'm so tired of having to run, run, run from giant predators," he seethed. "I hate being so small. And I hate never being able to finish a meal—I'm a mere exoskeleton!"

Through the long night, Crickwing's wing throbbed as he waited in his hideout.

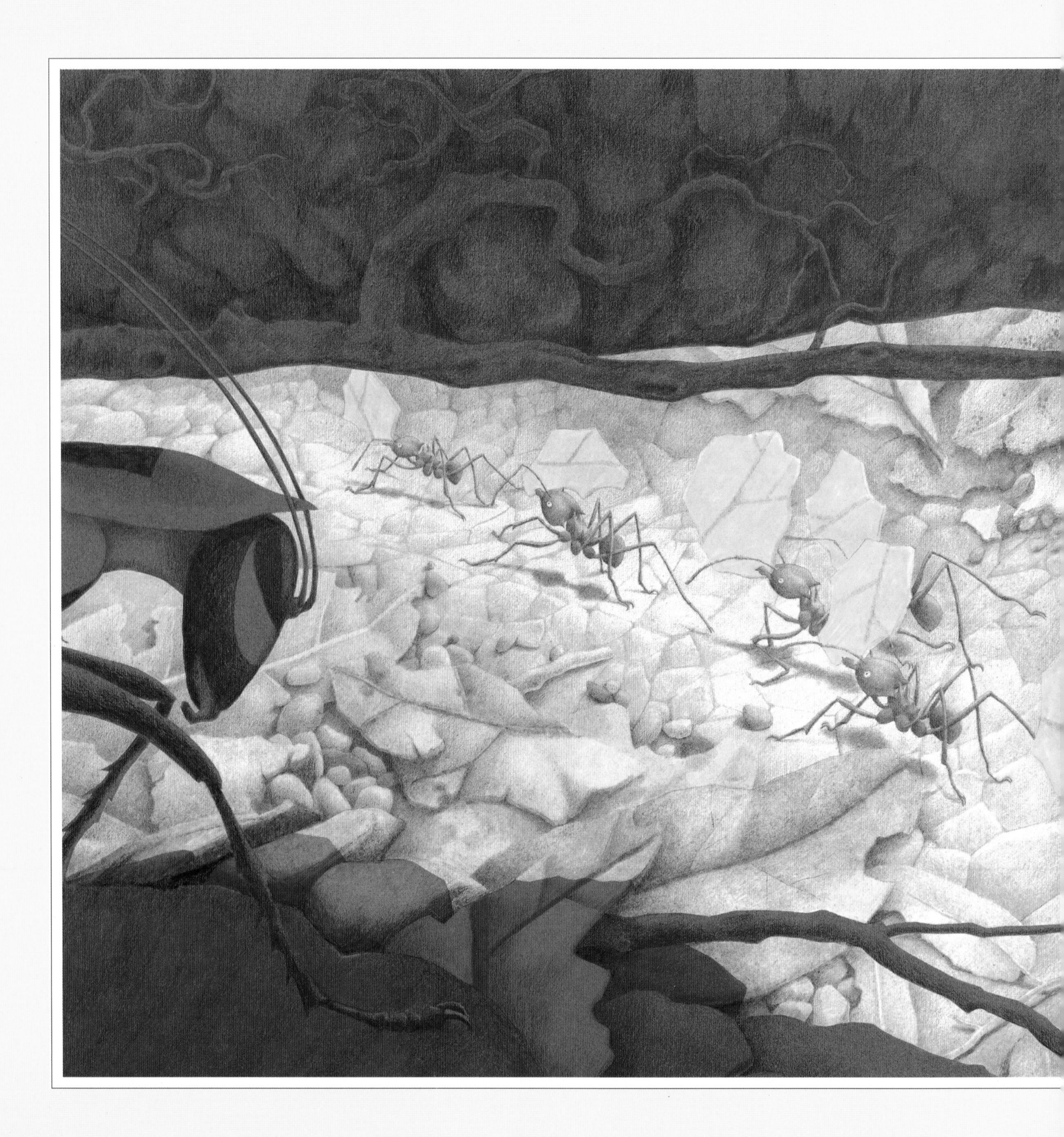

Many hours later sunlight streamed into his cave, and the leaf-cutting ants began another busy day. Thousands of the tiny workers carried large slices of leaves back to their colony. Crickwing, groggy and still angry, crept out for a better look.

"Ha! These guys are even punier than I am," he muttered. None of the ants seemed to notice him.

Crickwing inched closer. "There's something about these eensy critters that just bugs me. Why isn't anyone bothering *these* little twerps?"

He placed a spiny leg across the leafcutter path. "Well, let's see what happens now." He chortled. "Have a nice trip—see you next *fall*!"

Several ants stumbled, but then went back to work as if Crickwing weren't even there.

"This will get their attention," he growled, picking up a leaf from the path. The ant carrying the leaf hung on tight, which gave Crickwing a dastardly idea. He hung several ants from a vine, one by one, and watched with glee as their tiny legs flailed. Crickwing laughed so hard that he nearly forgot his aching wing.

That night Crickwing wolfed down a sweet flower bud, not even noticing its dazzling purple color. He had work to do.

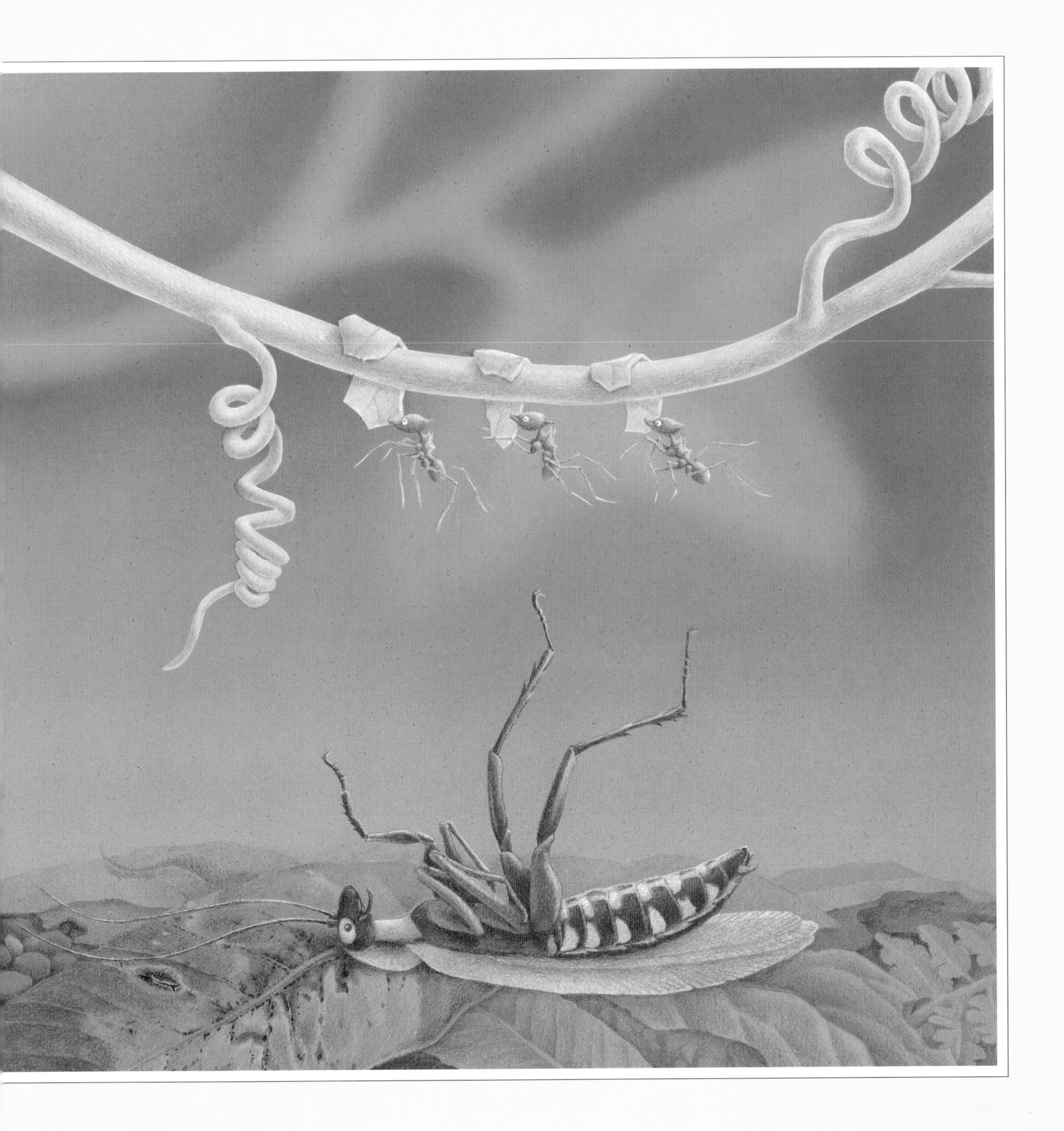

Right in the middle of the leafcutter trail, he dug a deep hole in the ground. Then he crouched behind a rock, waiting to see what the ants would do.

In the very early dawn, the ants rose as usual and went to work. When they returned, their cargo clamped in their jaws, they could barely see their way. They plummeted into the trap, piling into a great green heap.

"These muddling molecules are so easy to fool!" snorted Crickwing.

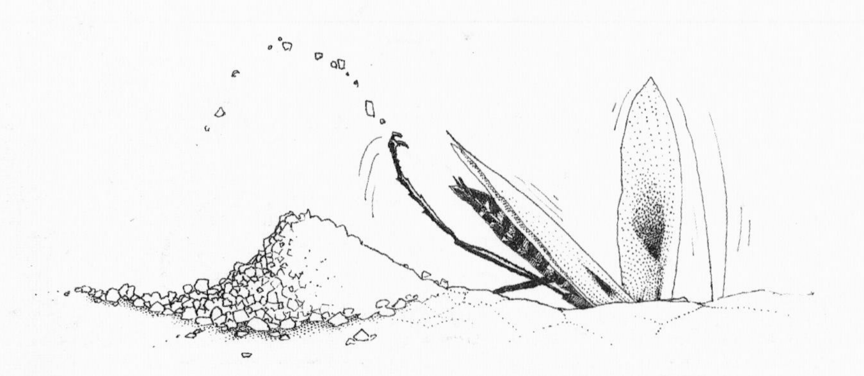

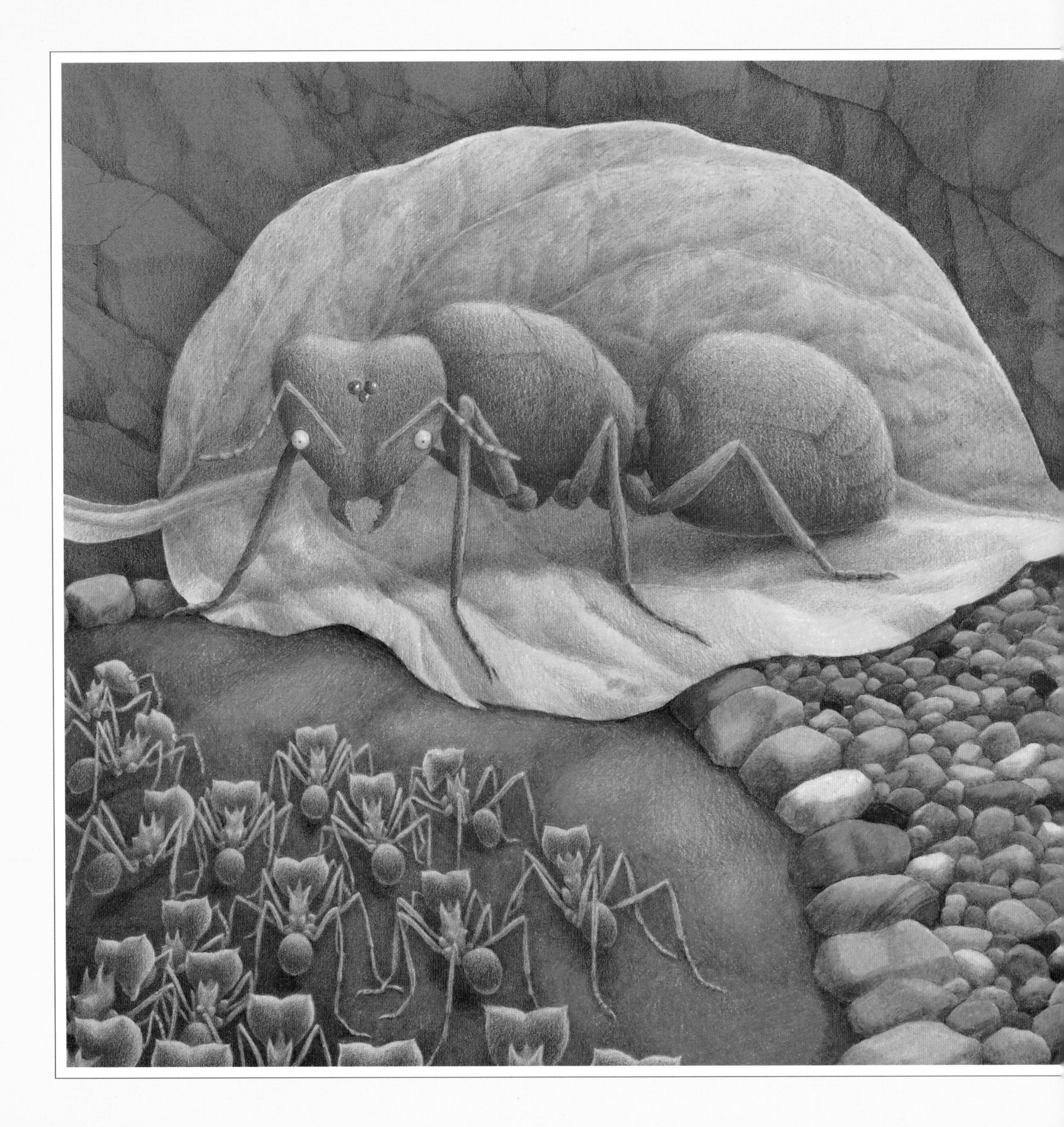

Back in the leafcutter colony, the queen of the ants called a meeting.

"This week's production is down!" she barked. "What on earth is going on?"

"It's a cockroach, Your Highness," stammered Terra.

"He's picking on us," added Gravel.

"No cockroach meddles with our colony. Seize him!" ordered the queen.

The next morning the ants found Crickwing fussing with his latest ant trap. He had no chance for escape as thousands of leafcutters swarmed over him, dragged him back to the anthill, and marched him down its dark, winding corridors.

When the tunnels narrowed, the ants crammed Crickwing through one final tight spot. *Pop!* His wing snapped back into place, and he realized that the throbbing ache was gone. Before he could give it another thought, the ants pulled their prisoner into a chamber and buried him up to his neck. For hours the whole colony filed by, whispering to one another: "How do you think he became so awful?" and "His mother must be heartbroken."

"That big oaf showed up just in time for the annual peace offering to the army ants," crowed the queen. "There's no way they'll attack us if we hand this hefty no-gooder over to them. Truss him up like the fat turkey he is and ship him out!"

The leafcutters bound Crickwing, hauled him back through the dim tunnels, and carried him up into the forest.

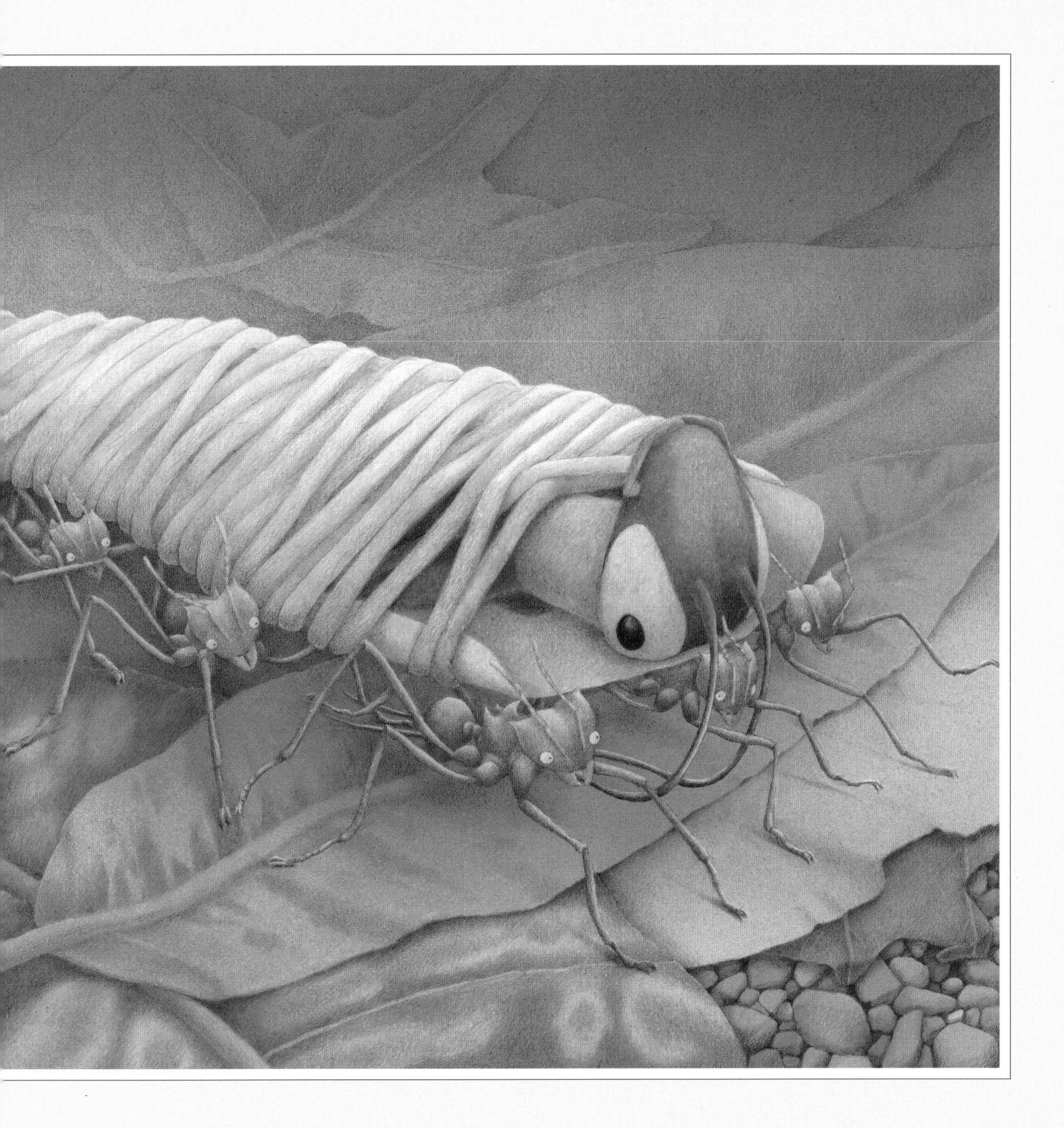

The ants hiked in silence for a long time.

"I can't do this," Eartha blurted at last.

"Neither can I." Terra shuddered. "Remember the giant beetle we brought to the army ants last year?"

"Yeah. They took him apart before we could even turn around and leave," quavered Gravel.

Crickwing gulped.

"Nobody deserves that, not even this big bully," said Eartha. "I say let him go. He never really hurt any of us."

"What will we tell the queen?" Terra gasped.

"And what about the army ants?" Gravel howled. "They'll level our colony!"

"I just can't watch them shred this guy," insisted Eartha. "We'll figure something out on the way back. Let's go!"

The ants released Crickwing and fled.

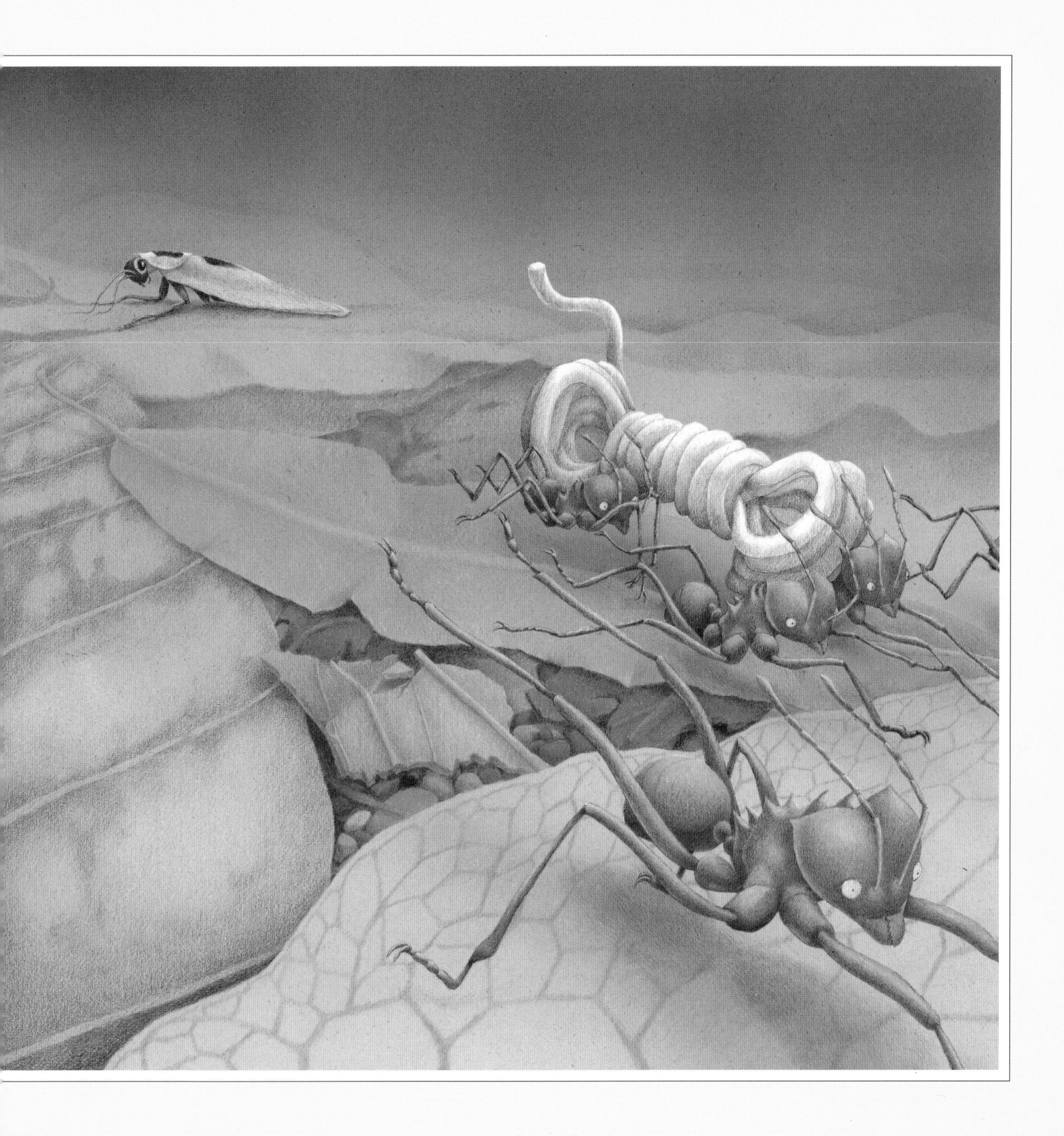

Crickwing was stunned. *The queen is going to have their heads! And the whole leafcutter colony is now in serious danger—all because of me.* Now that his wing no longer hurt, he could think clearly. *I have to do something, but what?*

And then Crickwing had a brilliant idea.

"Wait! Wait!" he yelled, racing after the leafcutters. "I can help! *Wait!*"

He described his plan, and the ants listened carefully.

"We'll have to move quickly, but if every ant pitches in, I think it'll work," Crickwing said.

"Can we trust this yahoo?" yelped Gravel.

"Do we have much choice?" snapped Terra.

"The plan is worth a try, and we'll do our best to win the patience of the queen," Eartha promised. "But we don't have much time."

"Jump on my back, all of you," said Crickwing. "I am one fast runner."

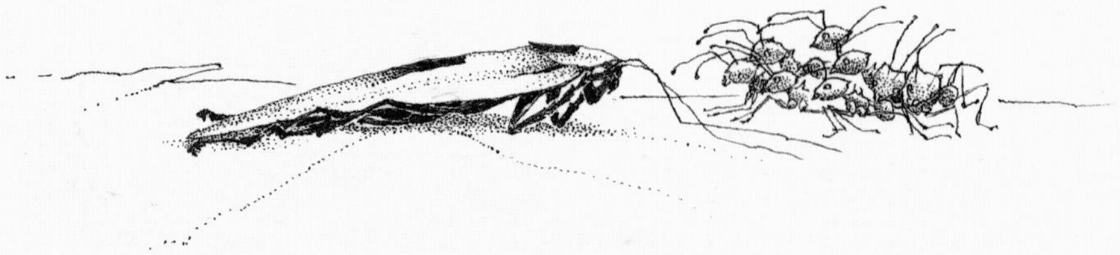

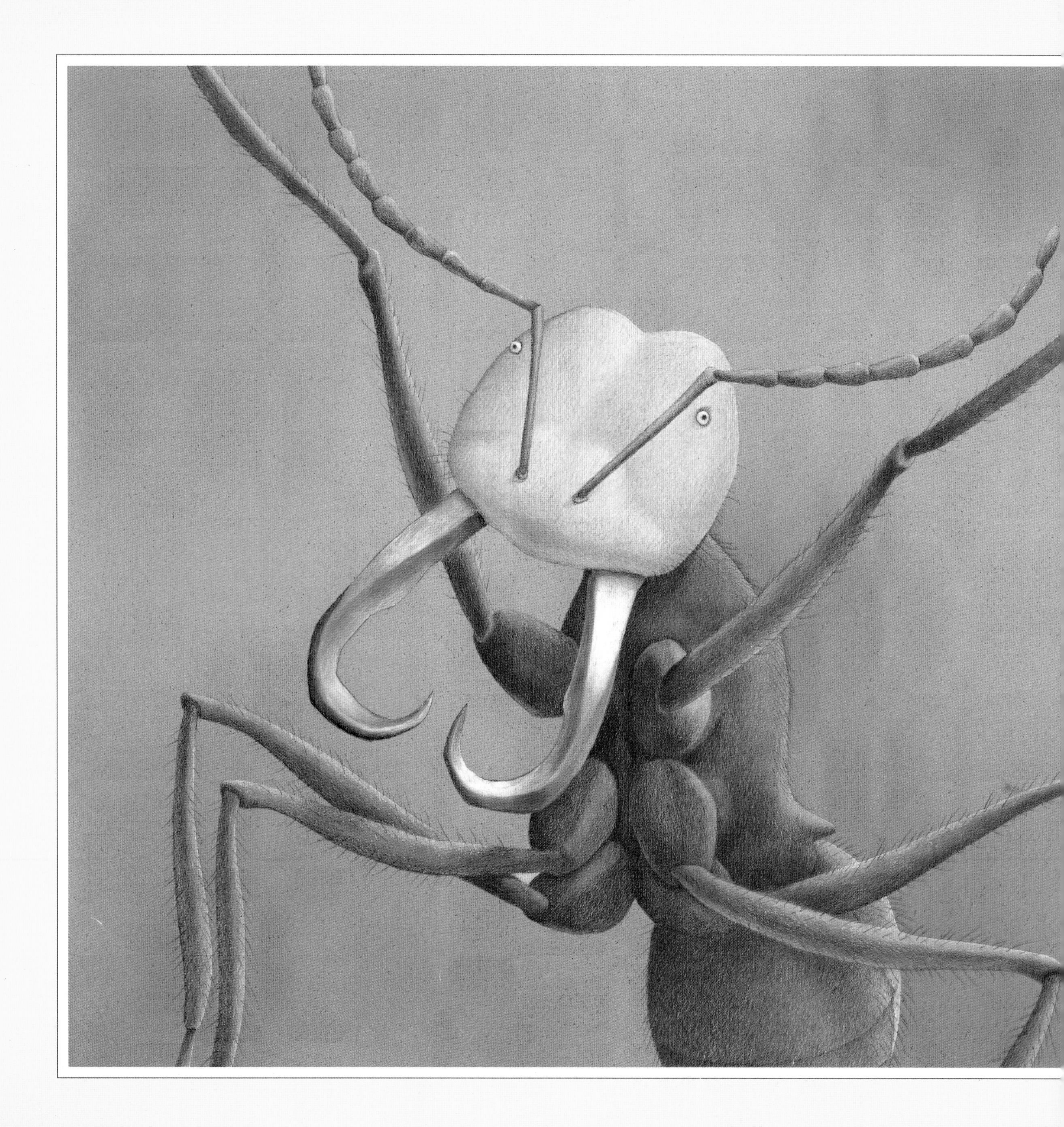

In a far corner of the forest, in the army ant camp, the lieutenant paced angrily. "Those leaf-eating fools are *late*!" she snarled. "If we don't have our peace offering by tomorrow at dawn, we march in and take what's rightfully ours."

As the hours passed, the army ants grew more agitated.

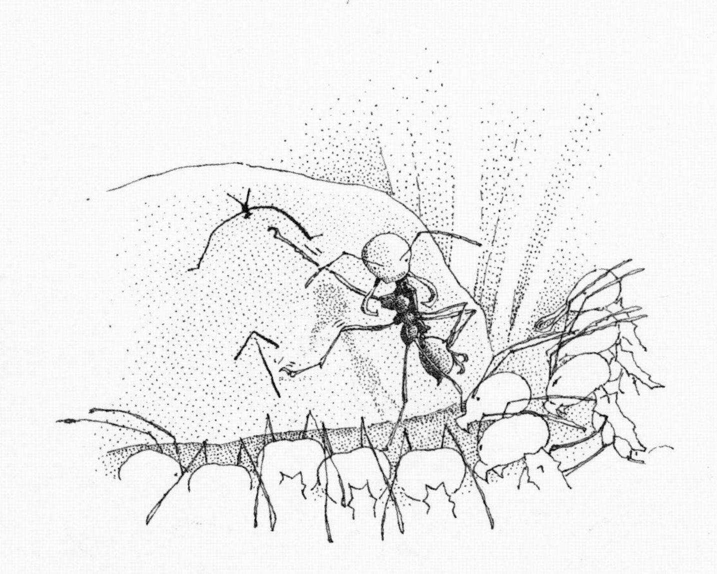

At first light, the army swarmed from its nest, ready for conquest. "No one!" shouted the lieutenant. "Absolutely no one keeps the army ants waiting!" They poured like an angry river down the trail to the leafcutter anthill.

As the ferocious ants turned the final bend, they stopped dead in their tracks. . . .

For a long, silent moment, they stared at the hugest, strangest, greenest anteater they'd ever seen. It loomed high over them, its terrible tongue dangling from its mouth.

The lieutenant's squeaky voice broke the quiet. *"Halt! About-face! Run awaaaaaaay!"* The army ants tripped over one another as they scrambled back toward their camp, none of them daring to look back.

Crickwing and the leaf-cutting ants peered from atop the leafy anteater's head, watching the warriors fade into the forest. They all held their breath until the entire terrified horde had vanished.

Then the queen approached. "I don't think we'll be seeing *them* ever again, thanks to you and your enormous sculpture, Crickwing," she said. "Or should we call you Straightwing now? We need someone to help us keep this anteater in order, so I hope you will decide to join our colony. And I hear that you're an incredible chef."

"Oh, I just like to play with my food," Crickwing replied. "And please, call me Crickwing. Your Highness, I would very much like to stay. The first thing I want to do is prepare a great celebration feast for everybody."

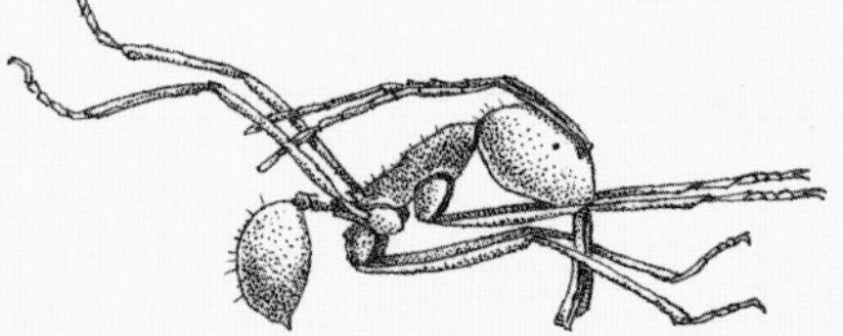

"Three cheers for Crickwing!" shouted Eartha. All the ants joined the cheer, then rushed into the forest. They gathered the brightest flower petals they could find and cut them into sparkling bits.

All night at the banquet, everyone threw flower confetti, danced the six-step, and sang until sunlight came creeping through the trees.

The queen peeked at the dawn and blinked drowsily. "I declare today a holiday," she yawned.

"Hear, hear!" said Crickwing.

And for the first time in colony history, the leafcutters took a day off.

COCKROACH NOTES

The world holds nearly 4,000 species of COCKROACHES, and new ones are continually being discovered. The differences between them are amazing. The variety in size alone ranges from a four-inch-long giant to a one-eighth-inch-long cockroach that hitchhikes on the backs of leaf-cutting ants. Some roaches are bright green and some look like ladybugs.

Some have beautiful stripes; others have bright orange rumps. One extraordinary cockroach is amphibious, which means that it spends much of its life diving in ponds and rivers, eating decayed leaves, dead fish, and algae.

Although cockroaches seem outrageously abundant, the Tuna Cave cockroach in Puerto Rico is in decline and may soon be added to the endangered species list.

Most cockroaches live in the moist, warm regions near the equator. Rainforests shelter thousands of species, which live everywhere from the floor of the forest to the canopy. Some cockroaches endure the extreme heat of parched deserts, while others manage to exist in frigid climates. Although few species are native to colder regions, humans have unwittingly expanded the insects' habitat into those areas by building places full of the warmth and food that help cockroaches thrive.

The common cockroaches that many people have grown to fear and hate represent just five species: German, Oriental, American, brownbanded, and smokeybrown. Globally, about fifty additional species are considered pests—less than one percent of the total roach family. The remaining thousands of species are content to live far from people, as they have for millions of years. Most eat fallen leaves and fruit, and their droppings help nourish the soil. Some pollinate flowers. Many jungle-dwelling animals consider the cockroach a delicious, high-protein snack. Considering how long these well-designed bugs have survived on earth, it is easy to see that we humans invaded the cockroaches' pantry long before cockroaches ever entered ours!

ANT NOTES

There are about 8,800 (and counting) species of ants in the world. Native species live nearly everywhere on the planet, except Antarctica, Iceland, Greenland, a Polynesian island, and other small islands in the Atlantic and Indian Oceans—and nonnative ants have migrated even to those regions. Ants are among the planet's best earthmovers. Their tunnel-building activity loosens the soil, making it easier for plants to grow. Many ant species help the spread of vegetation by dispersing seeds. Their underground food storage nourishes the soil.

A colony of LEAF-CUTTING ANTS can displace about 80,000 pounds of soil when building its massive nest. The nest's tunnels and chambers, as deep as eighteen feet underground, can shelter millions of ants.

One might assume that leafcutters gather foliage simply because they like to eat salad. Not so—leaf-cutting ants eat fungus, not leaves. In fact, they are very sophisticated farmers. The largest ants go out into the forest, where they use their sharp, powerful mandibles to slice off dime-size pieces of leaves. They return to the colony, where smaller ants take over and cut the leaves into even smaller pieces. The tiniest ants then cut the pieces further and use them to feed a fungus that grows nowhere else except in the leafcutters' underground caverns. The smallest ants perform complex weeding tasks and carry antibacterial agents to keep their crops productive and free of disease. The entire colony feeds on the nutritious fungus.

ARMY ANTS live in forests from southern Mexico to Brazil and Peru. These migratory warrior-like insects are known for their spectacular hunting technique. During a hunting march, hundreds of thousands of army ants swarm across the jungle floor, consuming every creature that they can capture.

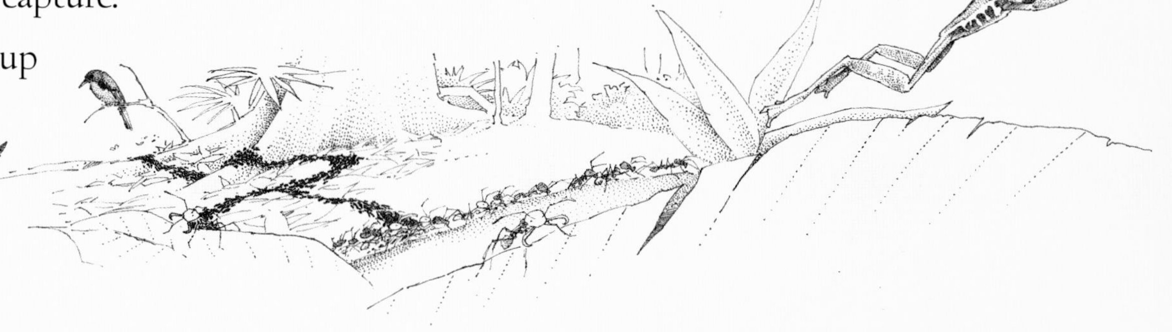

The huge band of ants stirs up everything in its path, including many varieties of insects; antbirds follow the army ants and gobble up the fleeing bugs. A certain butterfly follows the antbirds, feeding on the bird droppings. Many flies hover nearby, picking off any unclaimed prey.

As with many species of ants, army ants vary in size and color depending on their role in the colony and their stage of development. Most are hunters. The majors, large soldier ants that sport huge, swordlike mandibles, march on the sidelines to protect the hunters as they search for their quarry. Other workers help feed the majors, because their great jaws are adapted for fighting, not eating.

Unlike most ants, army ants do not build nests. When night falls and it's time to rest, the entire colony of ants gathers into one big clump, called a bivouac, usually protected by a tree. It takes a lot of food to feed a large army ant group, so they hunt daily. When it's time to raise their offspring, the ants camp for a while, using their bodies to shelter the queen and the young. When the new workers are ready, the army ants go marching on.

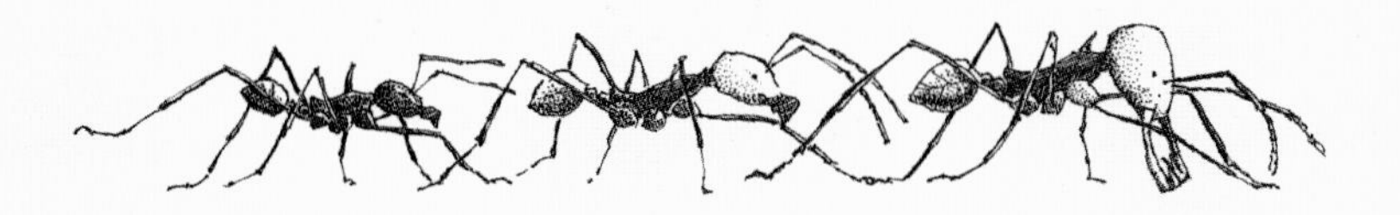

For information about permission to reproduce selections from this book, please write Permissions, Houghton Mifflin Harcourt Publishing Company 215 Park Avenue South NY NY 10003.

www.hmhco.com

First Voyager Books edition 2005
Voyager Books *is a trademark of Harcourt, Inc., registered in the United States of America and/or other jurisdictions.*

The Library of Congress has cataloged the hardcover edition as follows:
Cannon, Janell, 1957–
Crickwing/written and illustrated by Janell Cannon.
p. cm.
Summary: A lonely cockroach named Crickwing has a creative idea that saves the day for the leaf-cutting ants when their fierce forest enemies attack them.
[1. Cockroaches—Fiction. 2. Ants—Fiction.
3. Forest insects—Fiction. 4. Insects—Fiction.] I. Title.
PZ7.C1725Cr 2000 [E]—dc21 99-50456
ISBN 0-15-201790-9
ISBN 0-15-205061-2 pb

SCP 14 13 12 11 10
4500467504

The illustrations in this book were done in Liquitex acrylics and Prismacolor pencils on bristol board.
Display lettering by Judythe Sieck
The text type was set in Goudy Italian.
Printed in China by South China Printing Company Ltd.
Production supervision by Sandra Grebenar and Ginger Boyer
Designed by Judythe Sieck